Mike's Kite

by Elizabeth MacDonald
illustrated by Robert Kendall

ORCHARD BOOKS   New York

Mike was flying his kite on the hill beside the church near his home.

Suddenly the wind blew so hard that Mike had to hold on to the string with both hands.

The wind pulled the kite and the kite pulled Mike. It pulled him clear across the grass.

"Help! Help!" he cried.
"The wind is blowing my kite away,
and me with it!"

Two gentlemen walking their
dogs tried to help. They said:

The wind is strong,
and the kite is too,
but it's sure to come down
if we help you.

They held on tight to the string of the kite
and pulled very hard with all their might.
But the wind pulled harder....
It pulled them all the way down the hill to the park.

"Help! Help!" cried the two gentlemen, as they trotted past the swings. "The wind is pulling Mike's kite away, and us with it!"

Three nannies pushing baby carriages ran after them and said:

The wind is strong,
and the kite is too,
but it's sure to come down
if we help you.

They held on tight to the string of the kite
and pulled very hard with all their might.
But the wind pulled harder....
It pulled them over to the riding path at
the edge of the woods.

"Help! Help!" cried the two gentlemen and the three nannies as they sprinted toward the horses. "The wind is blowing Mike's kite away, and us with it!"

Four people on horseback chased after them and said:

The wind is strong,
and the kite is too,
but it's sure to come down
if we help you.

They held on tight to the string of the kite
and pulled very hard with all their might.
But the wind pulled harder....
It pulled them all the way through the woods
to the river.

"Help! Help!" cried the two gentlemen, the three nannies, and the four riders, as they sped along the path. "The wind is blowing Mike's kite away, and us with it!"

Five fishermen on the riverbank hurried to join them and said:

The wind is strong,
and the kite is too,
but it's sure to come down
if we help you.

They held on tight to the string of the kite
and pulled very hard with all their might.
But the wind pulled harder....
It pulled them right over the bridge to the farm.

"Help! Help!" cried the two gentlemen, the three nannies, the four riders, and the five fishermen, as they tried to avoid the cows in the lane. "The wind is blowing Mike's kite away, and us with it!"

Six farm workers left the
farmyard to help and said:

The wind is strong,
and the kite is too,
but it's sure to come down
if we help you.

They held on tight to the string of the kite
and pulled very hard with all their might.
But the wind pulled harder....
So they all raced down the lane toward the bakery.

"Help! Help!" cried the two gentlemen, three nannies, four riders, five fishermen, and six farm workers, as they sped past the bakery. "The wind is blowing Mike's kite away, and us with it!"

Seven bakers ran out of the bakery and said:

The wind is strong,
and the kite is too,
but it's sure to come down
if we help you.

They held on tight to the string of the kite
and pulled very hard with all their might.
But the wind pulled harder....
It pulled them straight down to the harbor.

"Help! Help!" cried the two gentlemen, three nannies, four riders, five fishermen, six farm workers, and seven bakers as they raced across the waterfront. "The wind is blowing Mike's kite away, and us with it!"

Eight sailors dashed after them and said:

The wind is strong,
and the kite is too,
but it's sure to come down
if we help you.

They held on tight to the string of the kite
and pulled very hard with all their might.
But the wind pulled harder....
It dragged them over to the town.

"Help! Help!" cried the two gentlemen, three nannies, four riders, five fishermen, six bakers, and eight sailors as they flew through the market. "The wind is blowing Mike's kite away, and us with it!"

Nine shoppers rushed to help them and said:

The wind is strong,
and the kite is too,
but it's sure to come down
if we help you.

They held on tight to the string of the kite
and pulled very hard with all their might.
But the wind pulled harder....
It swept them helter-skelter down High Street
and up the hill to the fire station.

"Help! Help!" panted the two gentlemen, three nannies, four riders, five fishermen, six farm workers, seven bakers, eight sailors, and nine shoppers as they trailed past the fire station toward the church. "The wind is blowing Mike's kite away, and us with it!"

Ten firemen stopped cleaning their engines and caught them
as they streamed across the grass beside the church. They said:

The wind is strong,
and the kite is too,
but it's sure to come down
if we help you.

They held on tight to the string of the kite
and pulled very hard with all their might.

And suddenly the wind stopped blowing.